Acknowledgments

This book is dedicated first to Shannan M. When the perfect storm first hit, she stepped up to offer her friendship and showed me the gift that I had been given. She is also the one who told me, "Share your unique situation and write a book." I hope that after all of the clouds fade away, the glimmer of friendship shines on.

Next, to Barb B, who has shown me what being a true leader really means. Thank you for weathering the storm with me, and all of its aftermath. Thanks for keeping your door "always open" so when I start to feel the storm clouds darken, I can stop in for a chat to brighten my day and to help keep me grounded. And of course, thanks for answering my never-ending myriad logistical questions with endless patience.

A special thank-you to Dr. NR and Dr. LH. Though you get paid to put up with me, you can't put a price on how much I appreciate your advice, discussions, and the extra effort you make to offer your professional wisdom to a "colleague."

To Mom and Dad, thank you for giving me a strong foundation of love and for always encouraging my dreams. Thank you for loving me despite, and because of, all of my differences. Mom, thank you for always trying to get me to see the sunshine in every situation. Dad, thank you for teaching me how to make up silly stories and songs and encouraging my endless imagination. There are now two other precious children whose lives are enriched because of the often unspoken lessons that you have both taught me. That legacy will continue through them.

To Shaena, my "Swamp Rat," who is beautiful on the outside and even more beautiful on the inside. You may not have come from one of my scrambled eggs, but I love you like you were my own (and I got to skip the puking, pooping, and slobbery stages!).

To Jacob, my Baby Skwid, who loves rainbows, dinosaurs, reading, snuggles, tickling, and silly jokes (he named Mo Bull "like the phone"). I see my imagination, creativity, and unique intelligence reflected in your big brown eyes, and the love I feel for you knows no bounds. You are my special Little Guy, and I love you just the way you are!

To Emily, my little Skwiggle, who loves lady bugs, tickling, snuggling, reading, giving slobbery kisses, and who has the cutest little witch giggle. I see my love of animals, my creativity, and my nurturing soul every day reflected in your beautiful eyes and in your warm hugs. The love I feel for you fills my heart with happiness. You are my little Baby Girl, and I love you just the way you are!

To Patrick, my FAS, the "Daddy Person" (you know I couldn't leave that out), my anchor in a churning sea, and my safe harbor. Our storm sometimes seems endless, but we have weathered so much more in the past decade that we should try to remember to hold on tight to each other and ride through these stormy seas too. I am sorry that sometimes I can be a pain in the "aspie," but you said, "I do," so now there is no refund policy! I love you so much as my best friend, my life partner, my soul mate, the father of our two beautiful little children, and the father of our grown-up daughter who reflects your inner resilience and compassion. In an ever-changing world, I hope we can find our way back to our teasing playfulness, your rock-steady patience, and my stronger resilience. Thank you for putting up with all my stuff and for sticking with me over the past ten years. I hope that I can soon find my place next to Floppy up on that great big, green box, but I will need your strength to help me get there! I love you with all of my heart and soul. Woozles!

Floppy Lop-Ears woke up to his buzzing alarm clock to get ready for school.

"*Buzz, buzz, buzz,*" he mimicked as he pushed the button to turn the alarm off, and then pushed it two more times just because he always did.

He jumped out of bed and put on his favorite soft blue pants and his snuggly warm red-and-yellow striped shirt. He liked to wear his fluffy red socks and his shiny black shoes.

"Shiny shoes, shiny shoes, shiny shoes," he said as he tied each shoe, just the way he did every morning. He liked how that sounded.

Floppy went downstairs to eat breakfast. He picked up his Chocolate Bunny Milk and took a sip.

"Good morning, Floppy," Mommy Lop-Ears said as she kissed him on top of his head.

"Good morning, Mommy," replied Floppy. "I'm hungry for a big bowl of Hunny Bunny cereal."

"I'm sorry, Floppy," Mommy said. "I forgot to get some at the store yesterday. How about some clover pancakes instead?"

Floppy got a funny feeling in his tummy, like it was becoming as hard as a stone. He *always* ate Hunny Bunny cereal for breakfast, in his green bowl with his green spoon.

"I have to have Hunny Bunny cereal!" he yelled. "I do, I do, I do!"

"Mommy makes really good clover pancakes," said Daddy Lop-Ears, taking a big bite of his pancakes.

"No!" shouted Floppy. "Hunny Bunny, Hunny Bunny, Hunny Bunny!" He was feeling like his whole body was tight and he was going to burst! He smacked his paw on the table and knocked his glass of Chocolate Bunny Milk right off the table. Floppy looked down at the puddle of milk on the floor and burst into tears. He started rocking back and forth in his chair.

"My milk, my milk, my milk," he sobbed.

Mommy and Daddy looked at each other with worried expressions. Mommy Lop-Ears put her paw on Floppy's shoulder.

"It's all right, Floppy," she soothed. Daddy Lop-Ears poured him another glass of Chocolate Bunny Milk. At first, Floppy was too upset to drink it, but then he sipped his milk while he continued to rock slowly in his chair. Floppy felt the funny feeling in his tummy begin to fade away.

Mommy looked at Daddy and said quietly, "I wish we knew why he gets upset so often whenever something changes."

"Maybe it's time to call Dr. Lamb and see what she recommends," replied Daddy.

Floppy had calmed down while drinking his milk. Mommy kissed his head, and Daddy helped him get ready for school.

• •

At school, Floppy went to his desk and pulled out his chair, and then he pushed it back in. He repeated this two more times, just like he did every day at school before he sat down.

"Chair in, chair out. Chair in, chair out. Chair in, chair out," he mumbled to himself. However, Mo Bull, who had a desk next to his, heard what he said.

"You are so weird," Mo told him.

Floppy didn't like when Mo Bull said things like that, especially when Floppy was only doing the things that made him feel calmer.

"Okay, class. Everyone sit down. Today we are going to start with math," Mr. Dill, the teacher, stated. Floppy smiled. He loved math and reading and spelling and science and … everything about school. Well, everything *except* how the other kids teased him sometimes when he mumbled things to himself, or when he didn't understand what they were talking about, or when he tried to talk to them and he said things that made them laugh at him.

At lunchtime, Floppy got in line for his food. He always ate the same thing. First, he picked up his apple juice. Then he picked up his tomato-and-lettuce sandwich. Last on his tray was his favorite, a bowl of green gelatin. He just loved how his favorite color shimmered and jiggled. As he reached for the green gelatin, he saw that there were only bowls of red gelatin! Floppy started to feel that funny feeling in his tummy again.

"Where is the green gelatin?" he asked the cafeteria worker.

"Sorry, no green gelatin today. Have some red. It's really yummy."

"What!" exclaimed Floppy. "I always have green gelatin! I *have* to have green gelatin! Green, green, green!" he shouted as he started to cry.

"Come on, crybaby," Mo Bull said from behind him. "Just take the red gelatin and hurry up! I'm hungry!" But Floppy wasn't paying attention.

"I always have green gelatin!" Floppy sobbed loudly. He started rocking back and forth, from foot to foot, as he cried and moaned, "Green, green, green."

"You are such a weirdo, crybaby," Mo taunted. "Crybaby, crybaby—"

"Mo Bull, that is quite enough!" scolded Principal Hedgehog as she came over to see what was causing such a disturbance. "Go eat your lunch," she told him.

"Come on, Floppy," Principal Hedgehog said, putting her paw on his shoulder. "I just happen to have an extra cup of green gelatin in my office, and you can have it."

Floppy sniffled and dried his eyes, and he slowly walked with Principal Hedgehog to her office. Just as she promised, she opened her desk drawer and pulled out a cup of green gelatin. He sat down on one of the chairs at a small table in the office. Then he opened his gelatin and scooped out a big blob with his spoon. The light made the blob of green gelatin shimmer as it jiggled on the spoon. He felt that funny hard feeling in his tummy start to go away as he rocked slowly and watched the green shimmery gelatin jiggle on his spoon.

Later that evening, Floppy was sitting at the dinner table. His carrots were in just the right spot on his green plate, and they were not touching his lettuce or his clover—just the way he liked it.

Daddy Lop-Ears said, "So, Little Guy. How was your day?" Floppy looked up quickly, then back down at his plate.

"They didn't have any green gelatin," he replied. "I have to have green gelatin with my lunch."

Mommy looked at Daddy, and then she said, "Yes, we know. Principal Hedgehog called us. She said that she was glad that she had some to share today. Wasn't that nice of her?"

"They should always have green gelatin," Floppy replied. "Will they get more before I go back to school? They have to have more green gelatin."

Daddy nodded. "Principal Hedgehog said that she would make sure they have green gelatin for the next time," he replied. Floppy smiled.

"They *have* to have green gelatin. I *have* to have green gelatin with my lunch."

That night, after he got ready for bed, Floppy tapped each of his toy dinosaurs spread out on his nightstand. He said good night to each one as he said their names. He always ended with, "Good night, Spinosaurus," because that was his favorite dinosaur. Then he crawled into bed and hugged his cuddly Snuggle Bunny tightly. Mommy and Daddy tucked him under the blankets.

"Daddy and I have been worried about how upset you get sometimes," said Mommy. "So we asked Dr. Lamb how we can help you feel better when you get upset if something changes. She arranged for us to visit Dr. Coon tomorrow."

"But I don't want to go to the doctor," replied Floppy, his voice quivering a little. "I'm not sick."

"There are different types of doctors," explained Daddy Lop-Ears. "Dr. Coon is the kind of doctor who talks to you and asks you lots of questions about yourself."

"I don't like shots," Floppy stated. "Is he going to give me a shot?" he asked.

"No shots," promised Daddy.

"Just talking," replied Mommy.

"Well, I guess that's okay then," said Floppy. Mommy leaned down and kissed him on the head.

"It will be fine," she said. "Remember, Daddy and I love you a big bunch."

"And we love you because you are special just the way you are," added Daddy.

The next morning, Mommy, Daddy, and Floppy Lop-Ears went to meet Dr. Coon. The doctor seemed very nice when he said hello to them and led them into his office.

"Nice to meet you, Floppy," he said. "Today we are going to play a lot of games, and I'm going to ask you a lot of questions to get to know more about you, okay?"

"No shots?" asked Floppy, trying to sound brave.

"No, I am not the kind of doctor who gives shots," he replied.

"Okay," said Floppy.

While Mommy and Daddy waited in Dr. Coon's office, he led Floppy into another room that was filled with all sorts of interesting toys. Floppy had a lot of fun playing while Dr. Coon watched him and wrote notes on his pad of paper. Sometimes Dr. Coon would ask Floppy about what he was doing, like why he was lining up all of his cars in a row. Sometimes he asked him questions about how his clothes felt, or things he liked to do the same way every day. He didn't even look in Floppy's ears or listen to his heart with a stethoscope. This was the strangest doctor appointment that Floppy had ever had!

When they were done, Dr. Coon said, "You did a great job today, Floppy!" They joined Mommy and Daddy Lop-Ears back in his office.

"Floppy, it was really terrific getting to meet you today," Dr. Coon said. "I have learned a lot about you." He looked at Mommy and Daddy Lop-Ears. "After spending a lot of time with Floppy today, I learned that he is very smart," Dr. Coon told them. Floppy smiled. "Floppy, do you sometimes have trouble fitting in with the other kids in your class or feel that you are different?"

"Yes," Floppy replied. "And they make fun of me and then I start to feel funny inside and then I cry. And then they tease me and call me a crybaby."

"Well," said Dr. Coon, "you *are* different than most of the other kids. But that's because your brain works a bit differently."

He looked at Floppy's parents as he explained, "Floppy has autism spectrum disorder, or ASD. There are many others who have this disorder, and each one may be just a little bit different. However, everyone with ASD has two characteristics in common. They have trouble talking with others, and they need to have certain routines or they become upset. Since some may have mild symptoms, while others have more severe symptoms, they refer to this disorder as a 'spectrum,' and those with autism spectrum disorder are said to be 'on the spectrum.'"

Floppy imagined himself standing up high on a big green box.

"I like green. Is the spectrum green?" Floppy asked.

Dr. Coon chuckled. "No, Floppy. Being 'on the spectrum' is just an expression. It is not a real thing."

"So," Dr. Coon continued, "one of the two things that those with ASD have difficulty with is being able to talk to others and to understand the things that are not said with words."

"What does that mean?" asked Daddy.

"Well," answered Dr. Coon, "we all talk with facial expressions, paw gestures, and the tone of our voices. Those with autism spectrum disorder miss all of this completely, so they do not notice many of the important parts in a conversation. This leaves them feeling left out, like they just don't get it while everyone else does." He looked at Floppy. "Or they say the wrong thing, and the other kids tease them."

"Yeah," said Floppy, "when other kids talk and laugh, I don't understand what's so funny. And then I try to say something too, and they all laugh *at* me."

"Exactly," replied Dr. Coon. He looked at Mommy and Daddy Lop-Ears. "You can help Floppy by using very clear language. He will find it difficult to understand phrases or slang words that do not mean exactly what the words suggest." Mommy and Daddy nodded, and Dr. Coon continued.

"Someone with ASD also has a really hard time taking turns in a conversation, and they can talk for a very long time about the things they're interested in. When someone with ASD gets a thought, they just have to share it right a—"

"I like dinosaurs," interrupted Floppy. "Spinosaurus is my favorite!"

"That's good to know." Dr. Coon chuckled. "Another common feature of those with autism spectrum disorder is the importance of a routine. They like to do certain things exactly the same way, such as getting dressed in a certain order or eating the same thing every day."

"I have to have green gelatin with my lunch," said Floppy. "They didn't have green gelatin at lunch yesterday. They *have* to have green gelatin. Principal Hedgehog promised there would *always* be green gelatin at lunch."

"That is a good example, Floppy," said Dr. Coon. "So, how did you feel when you found out they didn't have green gelatin?"

"I felt all hard inside, like my tummy turned to stone," Floppy answered. "And then I started crying, and I couldn't stop. And Mo Bull called me a crybaby."

"That sounds terrible," agreed Dr. Coon. "But having autism spectrum disorder means that you like things to be familiar or the same. When things suddenly change, it happens so fast that you cannot control all of those confusing feelings, and you have what is called a meltdown."

Floppy imagined himself standing in the cafeteria looking at bowls of red gelatin instead of green gelatin, while his legs started to melt like ice cream.

Mommy Lop-Ears leaned forward. "So that's why he was upset when we ran out of Hunny Bunny cereal, and he wouldn't just eat clover pancakes instead?" she asked.

"Exactly," replied Dr. Coon. "It is very hard for someone with ASD to change their normal routine without feeling upset. Of course, things can happen unexpectedly, but that is why it is important to learn what things upset Floppy the most. That way, you can learn to do things to help him calm down easier. You can also help to prepare him if you know there will be a change, so that he doesn't get upset with a sudden change to his routine."

"But he seems to get upset over small things," said Daddy, shaking his head in confusion. "How do we know when he will get upset, and how do we prepare him for changes when they might be so small that we don't even think about them?"

"First, for someone with autism spectrum disorder, like Floppy, *nothing* is ever a small thing!" replied Dr. Coon. "Things that may seem like no big deal to those of us without ASD can be a major source of overwhelming anxiety for someone like Floppy. It is very, very important for you both, as his parents, to make sure that you do not become upset or punish him when he becomes upset and has a meltdown. He cannot control these feelings, and it can be very hard or impossible for anyone with ASD to be able to explain why they become so upset. The best thing you can do is learn from the things that make him upset and try to remember to prepare him for those changes in the future."

"It seems so overwhelming!" said Mommy.

"It is not always easy," responded Dr. Coon. "But when he becomes upset, you can help him to calm down quicker by talking quietly to him. Most of those with ASD will also do things to calm themselves when they become upset or confused."

"Like what?" asked Daddy.

"Well, some like rocking back and forth," answered Dr. Coon, as he looked at Floppy, who was rocking back and forth in his chair. Mommy nodded. "Sometimes flapping their paws or making certain sounds is calming," continued Dr. Coon. "Most parents want to hug their children when they see them so upset. However, sometimes, those with ASD don't like to be touched or hugged, and this can cause a bigger meltdown."

"Oh, that's terrible!" exclaimed Mommy Lop-Ears. "I'm so glad Floppy doesn't mind a kiss on the head or a quick hug." Daddy nodded.

"Yes, everyone with autism spectrum disorder presents in different ways," said Dr. Coon. "Sometimes all of these different behaviors may look strange to someone without ASD. In school, other kids will make fun of them. Since ASD also makes it hard to have normal conversations with others, it is even harder for them to make friends, so they are usually isolated, even when they don't want to be."

"I don't think being 'on the spectrum' sounds like a good thing," said Floppy. "Can you give me some medicine to make me better?"

After a second, he added, "But no shots! I don't like shots!"

Dr. Coon chuckled. "Floppy," he replied, "autism spectrum disorder is not a sickness or a disease that goes away with medicine. It is how your brain works differently. It makes you unique, and sometimes that means you don't feel like you fit in. But there are also lots of things that are good about having ASD."

"There are?" asked Floppy.

"Yes," said Dr. Coon. "Like you can be really good at noticing little details about things, or you can get excited about something you like and remember a lot of facts about it."

"I like dinosaurs," said Floppy seriously. "Meat eaters are called carnivores, and plant eaters are called herbivores."

"That is very interesting," said Dr. Coon. "Yes, having ASD can make you very good at remembering things or make you very creative or give you a unique sense of humor. There are lots of other good things about it too."

"So I am special because my brain works differently," stated Floppy.

"That's right, Floppy," said Dr. Coon.

Mommy and Daddy Lop-Ears thanked Dr. Coon as they left his office.

That night, Mommy and Daddy tucked Floppy into his bed.

"Mommy and I think you are very special," said Daddy, kissing Floppy on his forehead.

"And we love you just the way you are," added Mommy as she kissed him on the top of his head.

The following day at school, Mo Bull saw Floppy and started chanting, "Crybaby, crybaby. Eat your green gelatin, you weirdo crybaby!"

"I'm different because I am 'on the spectrum,'" Floppy responded. "My brain works differently, and that makes me special."

"Yeah, es-*specially* weird," said Mo.

Floppy felt sad. *I don't want to be special anymore,* he thought. *I don't want to be 'on the spectrum.' I wonder how I can get off it?* He was glad that he had the next few days off school, so he could think about it some more.

Early Saturday morning, Floppy went outside after he ate his Hunny Bunny cereal and drank his Chocolate Bunny Milk. He liked to go to his playhouse where he could be all alone while he rocked back and forth and listened to sounds of birds chirping or the wind blowing. Today, he kept thinking about what Dr. Coon had said.

"I am not special," he said. "I don't *want* to be 'on the spectrum' anymore." He rocked and rocked, and he thought and thought.

Suddenly, he stopped rocking. He remembered something.

"When I was a very little bunny, I climbed high up in a big chair because I thought I could take a great big bunny hop right off it," he said. "I'm much bigger now. Maybe if I climb up really high in a chair, I can take an even bigger bunny hop right *off* the spectrum."

So with that plan, Floppy ran to the porch where Mommy and Daddy liked to sit in big rocking chairs and watch the sun set. Floppy climbed up in the chair. When he tried to turn around and stand up, the rocking chair rocked and Floppy flopped, landing on the floor of the porch.

"Owie," he cried, holding his knee.

Mommy Lop-Ears heard the *thud* and came running out to the porch. She saw Floppy sitting on the porch, crying. She scooped him up into a big bunny hug and kissed the top of his head.

"Let's take care of your owie, Floppy," Mommy said. She carried him inside and gently cleaned and bandaged his knee, then rocked him in her arms until he stopped crying.

"What happened, Floppy?" she asked. "How did you fall off the rocking chair?"

"I wanted to climb up high and take a big bunny hop so I could hop right *off* the spectrum," Floppy replied.

"Hop *off* the spectrum?" Mommy repeated. "Oh, my sweet bunny bun, the spectrum is not something real that you can hop off. You are so special, and Daddy and I love you just the way you are." She gave him a hug and added, "Promise me, no more climbing and hopping off things."

"Okay," Floppy promised.

That night, Floppy said good night to all of his dinosaurs, and Mommy and Daddy tucked him into his bed and quietly left the room. Floppy stared at his green glowing firefly night-light while he hugged his cuddly Snuggle Bunny tightly.

"Tomorrow I'm going to find another way to get off the spectrum," he mumbled to himself. And with that thought, he was soon fast asleep.

The following day, Floppy went outside and ran past the pond where orange, black, and white fish shimmered in the sun. Sometimes he liked to sit in the grass and watch them swim.

"Good morning, fish," he called as he ran across the yard to his playhouse.

Inside his playhouse, he rocked and rocked and rocked while he thought hard. Suddenly, he had another idea.

"Maybe if I dig a really big hole, I can crawl *under* the spectrum," he said. Then he took Mommy's shovel and went into Daddy's vegetable garden.

He dug and dug and dug until he made a great big hole and a great big pile of dirt—*and* carrot plants and radish plants and lettuce. He was covered with dirt from the tip of his long, floppy ears down to his fluffy white tail.

Daddy walked into the garden and saw the big pile of dirt and uprooted plants ... and Floppy covered with dirt.

"Floppy!" he shouted. "What are you doing to our vegetables?"

Floppy stopped digging and started crying, which made muddy streaks down his face. When he rubbed his face, he smeared dirt all over his favorite clothes, making him cry even harder. Daddy saw how upset Floppy was, and he took a slow, deep breath.

"Come on, Little Guy," Daddy said softly as he scooped him up, dirt and all. "Let's go get you cleaned up."

After his favorite clothes were in the clothes washer and Floppy was soaking in a nice warm bubble bath, Daddy asked him, "What were you doing digging up the garden?"

Floppy watched the rainbow colors glimmer in the soap bubbles as he replied, "I thought that if I couldn't climb up high and take a big bunny hop *off* the spectrum, than maybe I could dig a big hole and crawl *under* the spectrum."

"Oh, Little Guy." Daddy sighed. "The spectrum isn't a real place. Mommy and I love you so much, and we think you are special just the way you are."

• •

That night, Floppy lay in his bed, thinking about what he should do next. He was glad that tomorrow was Teacher Day at school, so he could stay home and think of another plan.

I just know I can figure out how to get off the spectrum tomorrow, he thought as he fell asleep, hugging his cuddly Snuggle Bunny tightly.

The next morning, Floppy sat at the kitchen table eating his favorite Hunny Bunny cereal with his favorite green spoon in his favorite green bowl. As he was drinking his favorite Chocolate Bunny Milk, he noticed Daddy opening a jar of clover honey. Daddy twisted and twisted and turned and turned the lid until he could finally lift it off the jar.

"That's it!" shouted Floppy. "Yip, yip, yippee." He loved saying that when he was very excited about something. Daddy was so startled that he almost dropped the jar of honey.

"My goodness, Floppy," he exclaimed. "What has you so happy today?"

"I have an idea!" Floppy shouted as he jumped off his chair and ran to the door.

"No more digging up the garden or climbing and hopping off things!" Daddy shouted after him.

Floppy was so excited. He just *knew* his new idea would work.

"Wooo, wooo, wooo!" he shouted as he ran across the yard and past the fish swimming in the pond.

"If I can't climb up high and hop *off* the spectrum, and I can't dig a hole and crawl *under* the spectrum, then maybe I can turn and turn and turn and I can lift myself right *up off* the spectrum," he told the fish.

Floppy stood in the middle of the yard and spread his arms wide. He started to twirl himself in a circle, spinning faster and faster and faster, until the pond and the green grass and the blue sky all blurred together. He turned and turned and turned so fast that he felt everything spinning, and he couldn't figure out how to get his feet to stop spinning, until ...

Plop! Floppy plopped right into the pond. The fish splashed as they quickly swam away. Floppy was dripping wet, from the tips of his long, floppy ears down to his fluffy white tail.

Mommy Lop-Ears heard a big splash and came running from the garden.

"My goodness, Floppy!" she exclaimed. "What are you doing in the pond? You are not a fish!"

She helped him out of the pond and into the house, where she gave him a nice warm bath. Mommy brought Floppy another soft shirt and pants to wear while his other clothes were being washed. But they just weren't his *favorite* clothes! He started to get that hard feeling in his tummy.

Mommy saw him becoming upset. "How about wearing your dinosaur pajamas, Floppy?" Mommy offered. "You love to snuggle in them every night when you go to sleep."

"Okay," said Floppy. He still felt a little bit of that funny feeling in his tummy because he was wearing his pajamas during the day, but they were soft and warm, and they *were* his favorite pajamas with the green dinosaurs on them.

Mommy sighed and kissed the top of his head.

That night, Floppy was snuggled all warm in his bed with his cuddly Snuggle Bunny while Mommy and Daddy kissed him good night.

"Floppy, why were you swimming like a fish today?" Daddy asked.

"I thought if I twisted and turned, I could lift myself right *up off* the spectrum, like when you lifted the lid off the jar of honey today," Floppy replied.

"Floppy," Mommy said, "you have autism spectrum disorder. It is not an actual *thing*. You cannot climb up and bunny hop *off* the spectrum. And you can't dig a hole and crawl *under* the spectrum."

"And you can't turn and twist until you lift *up off* the spectrum," added Daddy.

"I can't?" asked Floppy. "But I don't want to be '*on the spectrum*'. I want to be just like everyone else!"

"Floppy, you are *you*!" replied Daddy. "You are our special little bunny, and we wouldn't change anything about you."

"That's right," agreed Mommy. "We love you just the way you are."

The next day at school, Mr. Dill had a big announcement for the class.

"Everyone is going to pick something that they are interested in, and then they are going to tell the rest of the class all about it."

Floppy felt his tummy get that funny, hard feeling in it again.

That night, Floppy told Mommy and Daddy about the big announcement.

"What will I do?" asked Floppy nervously. "I don't want to talk in front of everyone. They will make fun of me."

"Just talk about what you love and forget anyone else is there," suggested Daddy.

"What about your dinosaurs?" added Mommy. "You love playing with them, and you know all sorts of stuff about each one of them."

"You are definitely the dinosaur expert in this house," agreed Daddy.

"I love dinosaurs," Floppy said as he looked at his nightstand covered with dinosaurs. He felt that funny feeling in his tummy fade away as he fell asleep.

On the following day, Floppy carried a big box filled with all of his dinosaurs and put it on the floor next to his chair at the breakfast table.

Daddy pointed to the box and said, "You can tell them all about the triceratops and his spikey tail."

"A triceratops has three horns on its head and a frill," Floppy replied seriously. "A stegosaurus has four spikes on its tail."

"Oops, my mistake." Daddy chuckled.

"I think you will do a great job today," added Mommy.

Mommy and Daddy Lop-Ears smiled to each other.

That morning in school, Floppy listened as the other kids talked about cars, butterflies, and robots. He had the box of dinosaurs next to his desk, but he held the spinosaurus because that was his favorite dinosaur. That funny feeling started to get bigger in his tummy while he waited for his turn. He rocked slowly back and forth in his chair while he stroked his fingers across the ridges of the sailed back of the spinosaurus.

"Rock-a-bye bunny, crybaby," whispered Mo Bull. Floppy tried to pretend he did not hear the taunt, and he rocked faster.

All too soon, Mr. Dill announced that it was Floppy's turn. Floppy got up slowly and picked up his box of dinosaurs. He put it down on the front table of the classroom and looked down at the spinosaurus in his paws.

He couldn't talk! His tummy felt so hard. He began rocking slowly from foot to foot while rubbing the spiny ridges of the sailed-back dinosaur. Some of the kids laughed.

"Freakasaurus," called Mo Bull.

Floppy felt that funny feeling in his tummy get bigger.

Mr. Dill scowled at the class. "Mo! It is very rude to tease others because they are different," scolded Mr. Dill. "Everyone has something that makes them different from everyone else, and we all need to respect others."

"Floppy has autism spectrum disorder, and that means his brain is unique," explained Mr. Dill to the class. "Sometimes it is hard for him to know how to have a conversation or how to handle change, but it also means that he has a different sense of humor, and he is very, very good at remembering things that he is interested in." Mr. Dill looked at Mo Bull again.

"Mo, if you can't remember to respect that everyone's contributions are important, then maybe I need to explain it to you again after school."

Mo Bull looked down at his hooves. "Sorry," he mumbled.

"Okay, then," said Mr. Dill. He looked at Floppy. "Whenever you are ready to begin, Floppy," he instructed.

Floppy felt the funny feeling in his tummy slowly get smaller. He looked down at his spinosaurus, and then he started reciting all of the things that he knew about it. At first, his voice was quiet, but the more he talked, the louder it got, so that everyone could hear him.

When he was finished with the spinosaurus, he touched its sail one more time, and then he put it back in the box and took out another dinosaur. He held up each dinosaur as he recited all of the facts that he knew about each one.

As he held up a long-necked dinosaur, he started to tell everyone about the apatosaurus.

Mo Bull called out, "Looks like a brontosaurus to me." Mr. Dill glared at Mo, and Mo looked down again.

"A brontosaurus is now called an apatosaurus," replied Floppy.

"Wow," said Finn Fox as she leaned forward on her desk to hear more. Mo leaned forward too. When Floppy was finished talking about all of the dinosaurs in his box, the class clapped and clapped.

"That was an excellent presentation, Floppy," praised Mr. Dill.

"Yeah, that was amazing!" said Billy Beaver.

Floppy smiled a very big smile as he carried his box of dinosaurs back to his desk.

At lunchtime, Floppy carried his tray of apple juice, a tomato-and-lettuce sandwich, and his favorite green gelatin and walked to his normal corner table where he always sat alone. As he passed by another table, Mo Bull called to him.

"Floppy!" Mo shouted. Floppy froze and started to have that funny feeling in his tummy again as he waited for Mo to tease him.

"Floppy," Mo said again. "Can you sit here with us and tell us more about dinosaurs?"

Floppy was confused. "You want me to sit here, at this table, with you?" he asked. "You just want to be mean to me, right?"

Mo Bull looked down and then looked back at Floppy. "No," he replied. "I'm sorry I used to say mean things to you. I love dinosaurs too, but I don't know as much about them as you do. And you remembered all of that stuff without reading it! That's so cool!" Mo said as he pushed out the chair next to him so Floppy could sit down. "Please sit here and tell us more about dinosaurs," he pleaded.

"Yeah, please," said Billy Beaver. "Tell me more about Tyrannosaurus rex! He's my favorite!"

"That was so amazing!" said Finn Fox as Floppy sat at the table. She smiled at Floppy and added, "It was like you could just read all of that stuff right off your brain. I wish I could do that!"

Floppy smiled and looked down at his green gelatin. He had a different funny feeling in his tummy, but this one did not feel bad. He started talking about T. rex. He even imitated T. rex stomping, which shook the table and made his green gelatin jiggle even harder. Everyone giggled, even Floppy.

That night, as Mommy and Daddy were tucking him into bed, Floppy was still so excited. He hugged his cuddly Snuggle Bunny tightly as he smiled at his spinosaurus, once again carefully placed back on his nightstand.

"You know," he told Mommy and Daddy, "I tried to climb up high and take a big bunny hop *off* the spectrum, and I tried to dig a deep hole to crawl *under* the spectrum, and I tried to turn and turn to lift myself *up off* the spectrum, but I think that I like being right where I am."

Mommy and Daddy looked at each other and smiled. They hugged him especially tight.

"You *are* different, but that is what makes you so special," Daddy said.

"And we love you so much, just the way you are," Mommy and Daddy said together, as they turned off the light and walked out of the room.

As Floppy lay in his bed, looking at his green glowing firefly night-light, he imagined himself standing high up on a big green box, surrounded by all of his dinosaurs. He smiled as he realized that that was just where he wanted to be.

(Disclaimer—Autism spectrum disorder is often a very controversial subject. In this section, I intend to provide some additional information based on my unique perspective. The hardest part of being a pediatrician coping with ASD is struggling to communicate clearly to educate parents and older patients without insulting anyone because I miss the majority of the unspoken parts of the conversation. While discussing my perspectives on ASD and some of the controversies surrounding this disorder, it is possible that some people will take offense to the information or viewpoints discussed. However, I intend only to provide information from my perspective as an adult coping with autism spectrum disorder, who is also a pediatrician.)

****

When I was a young child, I remember that there was a television movie about a toddler with autism. I do not remember much about it except that there was a child rocking back and forth and not interacting with his parents. Nowadays, autism is the subject of much interest, fascination, and controversy. It is the subject of extensive research involving genes and environmental factors that may work together or separately to create the brain structure and functioning that manifest as autism spectrum disorder (ASD).

In addition, there is extensive focus on reliably making the diagnosis earlier than ever. Whereas at one time, the diagnosis may not have occurred until preschool age or older, now current studies are observing behaviors of two-month-old infants to see if any of those behaviors can predict the diagnosis! Now, young children who are identified with ASD have numerous resources available to them, including speech therapy, applied behavioral analysis, individualized school programs, and other therapies that did not exist a few years ago, let alone decades ago when I was a child.

When I was diagnosed in May 2013, Asperger's syndrome was the name for the milder form of what was essentially autism. Soon afterward, the updated diagnostic manual from the American Psychiatric Association, DSM-V, was released. It combines several of these similar disorders (including Asperger's syndrome and pervasive developmental disorder) together into what is now known as "autism spectrum disorder." The term *spectrum* refers to the vast array of presentations and severity among those with this diagnosis.

So, What Exactly Is Autism Spectrum Disorder?

For those of you who have children, grandchildren, or other youngsters in your care with ASD, you may have already learned much about it from the developmental pediatrician or psychologist who diagnosed your child. Likely if you have a toddler, you have been asked questions at your child's routine well-child exams that screen for possible behaviors that require further evaluation or those where the pediatrician can provide immediate reassurance.

In order to qualify for the diagnosis of autism spectrum disorder according to the DSM-V, a person must have deficits in *both* of the two defining categories: (1) social communication and interaction, and (2) repetitive behaviors and restricted interests. Some degree of these deficits must have been present since early childhood. However, in milder forms of ASD, they may not have been readily noticeable until the greater social demands of school and peer interactions make them more obvious. The different deficits, either together or individually, cause some degree of impairment in daily function or in different settings such as work, school, or home.

"Deficits in Social Communication and Social Interaction" is the first major category defining ASD. It refers to the overall difficulty starting, maintaining, or politely ending a conversation. The "rules" of conversation—taking turns, understanding body language or facial gestures used to express interest or annoyance—are all lacking with ASD. Many people also take things very literally and do not understand common slang or idioms that mean completely different things than their words imply (for instance, "hangin' out," "just chill," etc.). A school-age child who "corrects" his or her classmates about the "impossibility" of a common slang phrase is quite likely going to receive much ridicule for this difference alone.

Some with ASD may also feel a strong need to say things as soon as they pop into their heads, not understanding "social rules" about what is appropriate to say and when to say it (if ever). Some people with ASD want to make friends, despite misconceptions that they are all loners. But when you do not know how to start a conversation with someone you want to make friends with, and you say something that is inappropriate, the feelings of humiliation and embarrassment can linger for hours, days, months, or even years!

A lot of us dwell on these social blunders or we keep trying to go over the conversations in our head, but we usually can't understand what we did or said that was "wrong." This creates a lot of anxiety inside. Sometimes this anxiety builds up so much that venting our worries happens whenever and wherever we happen to be at the time. Just being around other people usually causes some degree of anxiety, because there is a constant worry that we will say the wrong thing or that someone will be upset and we will fail to see it in the person's facial expression, body posture, or the myriad other nonverbal ways those without autism "talk" to each other.

For those of us who tend to favor perfectionism, frequently making mistakes can be a source of constant anxiety. Not being able to understand what we said or did "wrong" or being able to learn from our "mistakes" makes the uncertainty of any daily social interactions unbearable at times. Hence, many with ASD also find some form of calming techniques, from rocking or flapping behaviors, to just needing to flop down on the sofa in comfortable clothes and lose ourselves in a good book, computer game, or other hobby.

****

Suggestion: That reminds me of something I recently saw online, about some alternative medicine holistic doctor who treated kids with autism. The suggestion was to "never ever let the child be alone" or they will "slip into their own world." Just reading that made me cringe with anxiety.

Dealing with others, whether someone has mild or very severe ASD, is the cause of a lot of anxiety. We need to have time to ourselves to regroup, calm down, and *get away* from social interaction. It is important for those with ASD of all severities to be in therapies (scientifically proven, *not* "alternative or holistic") to improve social interactions in an attempt to function independently or at least minimize meltdowns in common social situations. However, to force *anyone*, whether that person has ASD or not, to always be with someone else who is constantly trying to engage him or her would make anyone go crazy! Even those without ASD like their "me time." Respect your child or other loved one who has ASD, and give him or her some time alone. As long as they are not harming themselves, *this is actually healthy and calming, a way to decompress from anxiety that, if left unchecked, can cause a major meltdown.*

****

Suggestion: Because those of us with ASD cannot understand the unspoken nuances of a conversation, it is important to prevent misunderstandings whenever possible. A louder tone of voice can be mistaken for being yelled at, when it may have been meant as an emphasis to the statement without anger involved. However, *since most of us with ASD have heightened sensitivity to criticisms (whether they are meant as such or not), many of the things said to us can be very hurtful* or cause a lot of anxiety to build up inside. For those with more severe ASD, it is especially important to speak clearly and literally and to avoid slang or other phrases that are common in casual speech.

Pay attention to the person with ASD, and if he or she seems upset by something you have said, or you need to say something with emphasis, make sure you also explain that you are not saying it with anger and that you are not upset or disappointed. *Having a loved one or someone you take care of who has ASD means learning to think ahead to what you want to say and how you say it.* When the person with ASD becomes upset (as we will inevitably get for some reason), ask what he or she is feeling (if that person can explain it), or talk soothingly to help him or her calm down, while you take notes on the situation to piece together what the trigger was.

Remember: Loving someone with ASD *doesn't mean preventing every future meltdown or misunderstanding,* but rather stepping up by *making your own conversations clearer,* by *not getting angry when there is that inconvenient meltdown* over something you consider small, and by *always sincerely trying to understand things from their perspective* in order to ease their inner anxieties.

****

"Repetitive Patterns of Behavior, Restricted Interests, or Restricted Activities" refer to a variety of characteristics that make up the second category of deficits defining ASD. Some behaviors can seem quite compulsive, such as the need to frequently check things over and over—for example, to see if doors are locked or an alarm is turned on. Other rituals may have to be performed while counting or they must be performed in groups of a certain number (such as flipping a switch on and off three times before leaving a room). Verbal phrases sometimes are repeated quietly or aloud while performing certain actions. While these behaviors may be similar to obsessive-compulsive disorder (OCD), they are also a key part of many presentations of ASD itself.

Intense focus, or *hyperfocusing* on a task, also occurs frequently, such as spending hours on a particular homework assignment, editing and reediting it. Unlike someone with an attention deficit problem, the inability to complete the task quickly is not due to a wandering mind, but one that is constantly picking apart and changing the assignment, trying to perfect it. This hyperfocus may involve a single area of interest, such as memorizing baseball statistics or being unable to stop playing a video game (this can be very bad if this fixation involves violence, death, or an obsession with a person leading to stalking).

Carrying out these behaviors can take so much time that they interfere with daily functioning (making one late for school or work, forgetting to eat, etc.). Other rituals can actually involve soothing or calming, such as rocking, hand flapping, staring at a moving object such as a spinning fan blade, etc. As I mentioned above, these are a part of decompressing the severe anxiety caused by confusing situations, change in a strict routine, or myriad other things that may not be obvious to someone without autism spectrum disorder.

****

Suggestion: The hyperfocus can be a good thing if it later leads to a career in scientific research, etc. However, *if you know someone with ASD who is fixated on death, violence, an imagined relationship with another person*, etc., it is very important to talk to the police, child protective services, psychiatric hospitals, psychiatrists, counselors, physicians, teachers, or others who are "mandatory reporters" in order to *get this person help* and prevent a rare but media-sensationalized national tragedy. (The Newtown elementary school shooting brings me deep, unbearable grief as a mother, pediatrician, and person with Asperger's/ASD). Thank God, this is rare!

****

The restriction or rigidity in daily routine that makes up the second category of ASD refers also to a particular way of performing certain tasks, a very selective choice of clothes, foods, etc. Any deviation from this routine leads to some degree of anxiety. At its worst, a meltdown occurs where the person is overwhelmed by conflicting and confusing emotions and anxiety. There is a sudden outburst that may include crying or screaming, isolating oneself from others, needing to perform calming behaviors, or, occasionally, violent acts such as hitting (especially if a severe lack of verbal skills prevents talking as a way to express these distressful feelings).

A meltdown is a very uncomfortable feeling inside, and it is *not* done by a child or adult with ASD to get his or her own way. It is more like a volcano of confusing thoughts and feelings from the extreme anxiety produced when expectations of some kind are suddenly not met. When this anxiety cannot be contained any longer, it has to have a way to decompress. As I mentioned, many of those with ASD will find their own way to calm themselves, and this actually helps vent the extreme anxiety that they are feeling inside.

****

Suggestion: For parents or caretakers of anyone with ASD who does not have the verbal skills or the insight to be able to explain what led to the meltdown, it would be a good idea to keep a journal. By writing down small details about the events leading up to the meltdown, you might start to see a pattern and figure out what the triggers are and be able to either avoid them or learn how to minimize them in the future.

Remember, what may seem like "no big deal" to someone without autism spectrum disorder, can be a major source of anxiety to someone on the spectrum. Autism spectrum disorder is *not* a lack of emotions; it is about having *heightened perceptions of emotions and sensitivities to many common physical factors.* Is it any wonder then that for people with ASD, the overwhelming onslaught of many confusing feelings, especially with no verbal way to express them, explodes in a volcanic meltdown? *The worst thing someone can do to the person with ASD, whether that person is a child or an adult, is to minimize the person's feelings, tell him or her to "just get over it," punish him or her, or act like he or she is just "spoiled" and trying to get his or her own way.*

****

And as a pediatrician, it is important to emphasize here: *NEVER, NEVER, NEVER, NEVER smack, punch, kick, bite, spank, or hit a child (or adult) with autism.* This *should never be done to any child,* but a *child with autism will not understand and this will not only be cruel, but it is absolutely child abuse!*

****

The heightened sensitivity with autism spectrum disorder extends to sensory inputs, such as aversions to certain sights (bright lights, certain colors), smells, or loud sounds. Aversions to the tastes or textures of food may lead to a rigid diet of very limited foods, which in turn can lead to issues such as abdominal pain or constipation. Tactile stimulation is also a common issue for many with ASD. This can include avoiding clothing that is scratchy or itchy, or having to cut all of the tags out of clothing. For some, just being touched by others can cause great anxiety. This obviously would be difficult for parents of children with ASD who are unable to cuddle their children the way most parents do. This form of aversion also makes routine visits to a doctor or dentist anything *but* routine. Relatives and friends who do not understand ASD may be offended by a child who has a meltdown over a hug or a tickle.

Of course, sensory inputs can also be the source of extreme fascination for someone with ASD. The feel of a soft blanket may result in a repetitive soothing behavior. Repeating phrases or sounds, especially when excited, can also represent this fascination. Children with ASD may not play with toys in a typical way, instead becoming mesmerized by watching the wheels spin on a toy car, for example.

Of course, it is often overlooked when discussing autism spectrum disorder that *there are actually many positive aspects about this disorder!* Yes, you heard me right! For instance, the intense focusing, or restrictive interests, can lead to focusing on a difficult or obscure scientific problem or a computer programming design. It can lead to new scientific discoveries, finding miniscule clues to the past in scientific fields such as anthropology, or even finding evidence to solve crimes in modern criminal investigations. Intensity of focus can also create the discipline needed to complete medical school or advanced education. Many famous people of the past, such as Thomas Jefferson, Sir Isaac Newton, and Albert Einstein, are now thought to have had Asperger's or some degree of ASD, and just look at what they accomplished. *Many traits of ASD that may be deficits in one setting can actually make that same person excel in another setting.*

As mentioned, "autism spectrum disorder" refers to a wide spectrum of various degrees of severity present among those with this diagnosis. Those of us with Asperger's syndrome generally now fit into "Level 1, Requiring Support," which is the mildest level of ASD. While using full sentences (and often, advanced vocabulary) to communicate, the rules of social engagement have noticeable impairments. Repetitive behaviors or other deficits may not be as noticeable in many situations, either because support systems are in place, or because *some people with mild ASD can suppress certain behaviors (at the cost of great internal anxiety) and unleash them later in a safer environment* (such as at home).

The moderate form, "Level 2, Substantial Support," refers to those who have more severe deficits that are readily apparent even with different supports in place. Language may include simple sentences or monotone voice patterns. Repetitive physical behaviors occur often enough to be readily obvious, and there are marked difficulties changing activities or routines (resulting in more meltdowns).

The most severe form, "Level 3, Requiring Very Substantial Support," is manifested by severe deficits of functioning and very limited social interactions or responsiveness to others. Speech is also severely limited to few, isolated words or there may be "parroting" of words or phrases of others, without any indication of understanding. Repetitive behaviors are almost constant, and major distress occurs at any alteration from normal, very rigid routines. However, because they lack sufficient verbal ability, the *source of this distress takes quite a bit of detective work on the part of their loved ones* to find the pattern of events that trigger the often frequent meltdowns.

****

What Causes Autism Spectrum Disorder?

This is an area of intense research. There have already been genes identified that directly or indirectly lead to autism spectrum disorder. Environmental factors that may influence these genes to produce the changes in the brain that present as ASD are constantly being evaluated. *Since there is such a broad presentation of people with this disorder, it is impossible to find one factor* that can account for every case.

One thing that is known—and I have to mention it, just to be clear—is that *autism spectrum disorder has been scientifically proven to not be caused by vaccinations of any kind, nor is it caused by "overwhelming the body" (giving too many vaccines at one time at a very young age).*(See the reference list that follows.)

After my diagnosis, it occurred to me that the *vaccine debate is primarily parents of children with autism versus the scientific community.* I wondered why *I had never heard about a person with ASD who has voiced an opinion regarding the vaccine debate* (at least not to my knowledge). That led me to the *realization that I am indeed in a unique position since I represent both sides of this issue: a pediatrician and a person who has autism spectrum disorder.*

As a pediatrician, I learned the importance of vaccinations to prevent infections that can lead to lifelong tragic complications or death. *Even now that I know of my diagnosis, I fully support vaccinating all infants and children on time at the recommended age and with all of the recommended vaccines.*

As someone on the spectrum, I was fully vaccinated as a child. Now, before some of you say, "Well, there you go! That's how she got it!" pause for a second to remember one argument that was strongly voiced by a celebrity, insisting that there are "too many" vaccines today and this surely led to autism. The idea was that, before the mid-1980s, there were far fewer vaccines, and this was better. Well, my parents made sure that I got all of my vaccines as an infant and young child, before 1980, and yet I have autism spectrum disorder!

Many of you are now probably screaming, "See, she just *proved* that *no* vaccines are safe!" But consider this: I have two young children, and as a pediatrician and prior to my diagnosis, *I was adamant that both of my children receive every single recommended vaccination on time.* They are both past the age where autism should have been detected, and they do not have any characteristics of autism spectrum disorder.

Today, *even with my diagnosis of autism spectrum disorder,* if I had to do it all over again, *I would not for one single instant hesitate to vaccinate my children out of some misguided fear that vaccines are what caused my autism spectrum disorder.* In addition, *I have never once wished, even for a second, that my parents had never had me vaccinated all those years ago.*

If one continues thinking that vaccines or "overloading" the body with too many vaccines given at a very young age is the cause of autism, then *it would be logical to conclude that, given the combination of vaccinations* and *the strong genetic component from a mother with ASD, if anyone were going to get autism spectrum disorder, then my two children should have developed it for sure.* But neither one of them has ASD. Therefore, my perspective as someone who actually *has* autism spectrum disorder *and* who also happens to be a *pediatrician* is *in complete support of all vaccinations on time at the ages recommended in the standard schedule.*

Even though by now some may have been offended by what I have written, I nevertheless find it imperative to provide one final argument for consideration about why vaccinations at their recommended ages are so important.

During my pediatric emergency medicine career, I have had experience treating children with diseases and their devastating complications that are now preventable with vaccinations. *A sad irony in the vaccination debate is that the majority of parents who refuse to vaccinate their children have never seen the tragic consequences of those preventable diseases on children who are helpless to protect themselves.* While in training, it was fairly common to diagnose young infants with bacterial infections in their blood (septicemia) and/or in the fluid surrounding their brain and spinal cord (meningitis), and these infants were usually quite ill. Those who survived were often left with some degree of brain damage. The *pneumococcal vaccine was not available at that time* (pre-1999), yet since it has been on the recommended vaccination schedule, I have never again seen another case of pneumococcal meningitis. In fact, the entire evaluation of infants and toddlers with fever has also changed since the rate of this bacterial infection in the blood has dropped from an average of eight out of every one hundred children with fever (in the 1990s) to the current rate of less than eight for every *one thousand* children with fever! *Less unnecessary blood tests* means lower costs and most importantly, *less pain for the child*—all because of *a very successful vaccine!*

Varicella seems to be the one vaccine that many think is unnecessary, and these parents and guardians are willing to let their kids get the chicken pox virus because they believe that it is "no big deal." Sadly, they have never seen a child with a severe bacterial infection that developed in the chicken pox blisters. One unvaccinated ten-year-old suffered from such a severe infection that it invaded her bloodstream and multiple organs, causing shock that almost killed her. While she was fighting for her life, her father brought all of her siblings into the pediatric clinic to get them vaccinated. Luckily, her parents did not have to face a lifetime of guilt that their initial decision not to vaccinate had caused the death of their child. As a parent, there could not be a worse burden imaginable!

All pediatricians have seen the effects of these diseases. Many older pediatricians practicing before the 1980s have seen far worse diseases that were unheard of in my training due to the development of new vaccinations (*Haemophilis influenza type B*, or "HiB"). My pediatric emergency medicine experience has put me in the position to treat children in serious or critical condition, so I have seen some of these preventable diseases at their worst. That is the main reason why I am so passionate and dedicated to educate parents and guardians to vaccinate their children on schedule. *You just never know!*

To play devil's advocate, consider this final plea: suppose you believe that vaccines, or the recommended schedule of vaccines, cause autism or some other disorder. I ask you, *which is worse: a living vaccinated child with autism or an unvaccinated child who suffered severe complications and died as a result of what could have been a preventable infection?*

Resources

While this book is not meant to be a scientific paper or textbook, I nevertheless am providing some credible sources of further information. I also issue this warning: *Beware of what you read in cyberspace.* People with no scientific knowledge or understanding of how to interpret scientific research papers will misunderstand and misinterpret scientific findings and use them in ways that are *not factual*!

www2.aap.org/immunization   The American Academy of Pediatrics site for parents. This provides a lot of information about vaccines in much greater detail.

Autismspeaks.org   This is a great resource for all things about ASD, political action, ABA therapy, etc.

CPSIA information can be obtained
at www.ICGtesting.com
Printed in the USA
BVOW10s1136250816

460086BV00016B/160/P